I0445368

OFFICE SEX COLLECTION
EXPLICIT DIRTY EROTICA SHORT STORIES

DANIKA FALLS

plicit Press

CHAPTER 1

A CLASS ACT (OFFICE SEX)

LAUREN BALLARD'S breasts swayed back and forth as Jared Booker fucked her from behind. They were having one of their late-night work meetings and they sure were working hard. As colleagues in the legal firm of Anders & Brentwood, they had been immediately attracted to each other and held each other in high regard professionally.

Jared was Lauren's junior by ten years, but Lauren was beautiful, talented, and an awesome fuck buddy. She was wild, sensual, and had a mouth like a sailor. Jared smacked her ass, leaving a red mark behind as he drove into her cunt. She was wet and hot and Jared clenched his teeth to concentrate on not cumming yet.

It was always that way with Lauren. She drove him crazy and knew how to make him hot. On this particular occasion, Lauren had stood up from the conference table where they worked and stretched. Her breasts strained at her blue blouse, her nipples clearly outlined. She fixed a look at Jared and then went to close the blinds of the conference room.

Slowly she'd unbuttoned her blouse, exposing a

sapphire blue bra and a flat stomach. She took off the blouse, hanging it carefully over the chair next to hers. Jared's gaze followed the movements of her fingers as she unzipped her skirt and stepped out of it. Soon there wasn't a scrap of clothing on her and Jared's eyes raked over her sleek, naked form.

She kept her bush trimmed, but didn't shave, something that pleased Jared. He liked a little hair and Lauren's was soft. Her full, dusky pink-tipped breasts moved a little as she walked to the end of the table where Jared sat. She leaned against the table and then scooted back to sit on it right in front of him. Lauren spread her legs and leaned forward to kiss him.

At first, her kiss was soft and gentle, teasing. Then she grew more insistent, opening her mouth and darting her tongue out to meet his. She took one of his hands and drew it towards her pussy. Jared did as she wanted. He stroked her soft pussy lips, rubbing his palm over it and then sliding his fingers along her slit. At the bottom of it, Jared found dampness; a sign of Lauren's horniness.

Jared slid two fingers inside Lauren. He placed the pad of his thumb on her clit and began sliding in and out of her cunt. Lauren moaned and leaned back on her hands, spreading her legs farther apart. Jared moved his arm faster, his thumb hitting Lauren's clit and rubbing her G-spot with his fingers. Lauren moaned and her legs began to shake. She had been horny all day and couldn't help but be incredibly turned on.

She arched her back as she came, sweet ecstasy coursing through her body. The orgasm went deep and Jared felt her pussy clench around his fingers. His cock, already halfway hard, suddenly roared into full life. He withdrew his fingers and stood up. Lauren was on him immediately, undoing his pants and pulling them down.

She'd taken his cock in her hands and worked it, enjoying the hard length of it. Jared had a big cock and Lauren wanted to taste it. She flicked her tongue around the head and teased the hole there. Jared buried his fingers in her copper hair and pulled her head forward. Lauren smiled and then took him deep, the head of his cock touching the back of her throat.

She drew back, sucking hard and grasping his dick around its base and playing with his balls with her opposite hand. His balls were firm and full and she loved feeling the weight of them in her hand.

Jared growled as she sucked his cock. She made him rock hard and made him feel so incredible. She licked, sucked, and teased until Jared couldn't take any more.

He took off the rest of his clothes and then laid her back on the table. He wasn't gentle when he thrust inside of Lauren and she didn't want him to be. She wanted him to attack her like a stag in a rut and fuck her cunt like there was no tomorrow. Jared had delivered, pounding at her and twisting her nipples. Lauren held onto his strong shoulders, urging him on.

Jared felt her orgasm begin and moved faster, wanting it, forcing it. Lauren cried out in her slightly husky voice as she climaxed. She shuddered with pleasure and her fingers closed almost painfully over Jared's shoulders.

Jared stopped when her climax was over and then pulled her off the table. Roughly, he turned her around and forced her towards the table.

"Bend over, slut," he said.

"All right," Lauren agreed with a smile. She liked it when Jared got rough.

She leaned forward, gripping the table tightly. Jared slapped her ass and ran his hands over her body. She felt incredible to him, firm and yet soft. Then he nudged her feet apart so that her pussy was spread open. Jared smacked his cock against Lauren's rounded cheeks and then guided it inside her cunt. She was slick and so hot inside. Jared had sucked in a breath at how good she felt.

And now as he rammed into her from behind, Jared fought the urge to cum. Lauren always drove him quickly to that point. To distract himself, he leaned forward and grabbed Lauren's tits, playing with her nipples. Lauren moaned as Jared's attentions caused an intense pleasure to resonate all through her body.

An orgasm built within her and she whimpered as it overtook her. Her whimper soon grew in volume into a crescendo of bliss. Ripples of her pleasure stroked Jared's dick and he banged against her harder, thoroughly enjoying the fact that he gave Lauren intense orgasms. She'd told him what a good fuck he was and it always made him happy to hear it.

He humped her, feeling his own orgasm closing in. He wasn't going to deny it this time. His groin clenched as his cum began spurting deep inside of Lauren. A guttural growl issued from Jared's throat as a powerful climax surged through his hard body. Lauren felt Jared's hands grip her hips tighter and his hot cum shooting into her and reveled in it.

Jared's orgasm was long-lasting and he couldn't move while it was happening. When it was over, he stood panting for several moments. Then Lauren straightened, breaking their contact, and turned around to look into his beautiful blue eyes. She smiled up at him and then kissed him.

"Well, that was certainly a...productive night of work, wouldn't you say?" Jared grinned down into her lovely green eyes. "I concur, counselor."

CHAPTER 2

IN DUPLICATE... (COPIER CATS!)

JOE AND ALEX went to college together and so they were very happy to receive the same internship. And when their first assignment is with a hot New Yorker named Anna, they've really struck gold. The three have been pushing their project late into the night for about two weeks, determined to impress. But their heads feel set to pop, and they are tired and out of ideas. Out of sheer frustration, all three of them have already kicked the copier a few times, the sound of it on standby, an incessant buzzing, driving the trio crazy.

Anna gets more coffee, although she is already sure that it won't help. It's way past midnight on a Friday, and they would all rather not be there. But this is what they signed up for. Joe's eyes are starting to close. He hates it when he has no ideas. Alex is doodling on his note pad hoping that something is going to fall from the sky. After another half hour, none of them have even touched their coffee.

When Anna takes off her shirt and tosses it on the chair next to her the men are privy to the sight of her perfect breasts under her vest. It's a light-colored, perfectly acceptable Chanel top that works as well on its own as it did with the shirt and blazer on. Joe and Alan try in vain to look through her top, making out the outline of her nipples as she redoes her ponytail. The three of them get up and pace the length of the room, not speaking, looking at the work on the tablet they've already done. They are so close to finishing, but the ideas just won't come.

Joe and Alan allow their minds to wander. This wandering leads to rather large bulges in their pants. They go and stand near the window, facing out into the city skyline. They exchange looks and then point at their own bulges so that they both know what the other is thinking. Then they look at Anna as she tries again to draw ideas from her pen. Occasionally she puts the pen in her mouth and both men wish that it was their dicks sliding between her glossy lips.

It isn't long before Anna senses the gazes coming at her and she doesn't look back at them. She just enjoys the unspoken attention for a moment. It's that time of the morning when sex is the easiest thing to think of. And as a true New Yorker, Anna can imagine without a reservation being fucked by these two boys from Chicago. After a few minutes of letting this thought play around in her head, she decides 'what the fuck...'

She goes to the window and stands between Joe and Alan. She places a hand on both men's asses and they look from her to each other. Anna gives the firm muscles a good squeeze just to confirm with the two that it's time for a fun break. They've often joked about fucking, but none of them ever took it seriously. But right now, it's as good a thing as any, no work being done in the boardroom.

Anna is pulled to face Joe, him being the more assertive of the men. Alan comes up close behind her and rubs his erection against her ass. Anna rubs her fingers along the line of Joe's cock, as he too is hard under his pants. The two men warm themselves against Anna and then ease her to her knees, not wanting to waste too much time in case she changes her mind.

She works on Joe's pants just because he is positioned in front of her. Alan gets his own pants undone and pulled down to his knees. Anna gets Joe's pants to his knees after he helps with the belt buckle. Alan comes around to stand next to Joe. He isn't going to risk missing out on any of the action.

Joe can't help but give a few wolf whistles as his cock goes into Anna's mouth. She takes it all the way down and then lets it out. Then she licks the tip of it, holding it in her hand so that she can point it towards her mouth. Alan is moving even closer now, wanting the same treatment as soon as possible. He doesn't have to wait long. After licking and sucking Joe for a minute, she pulls Alan's dick into her mouth.

After giving a decent amount of mouth time to the men whose eyes are heavy with gratitude, she gets onto her feet. She unzips her skirt and removes it carefully. Joe helps with her bra and Alan is on his knees freeing Anna from her panties. Now she is naked save for her heels. She is so happy that she didn't put pantyhose on today or she would have lost this kinky naked-in-my-heels moment.

She walks over to the table, leaving Joe standing and Alan still on his knees. The men watch her move and then bend suggestively over the table. Then Alan is on his feet and they both go over to Anna, standing on either side of her and running their hands up and down her back, and then each of them rubbing one of her ass cheeks, and then going all the way down her thigh. She parts her legs so that as they rub her inner thigh they have access to her cunt, which they graze on the way up.

Anna places her palms on the table and forms a diagonal with her chest. Hands land on her breasts as the men come in closer to explore more of her body. They squeeze her tits hard and then soft, and then they pull on the perky pair before playing with her nipples. Anna's pussy is aching already, throbbing madly between her legs, wanting to be touched.

Alan stands with his ass against the table now and brings Anna over so that she is in front of him. Joe is behind her, pulling her towards him slowly until she is sliding Alan's cock into her mouth. She is really enjoying the taste of Alan's cock, and also the fingers that are pulling on her clit.

Then suddenly, Joe's mouth is on her cunt. She doesn't know how he has positioned himself, but it feels like he is upside down.

Then Joe is fingering her cunt again, his thumb testing her asshole. He drops some spit on it and soon he is fingering both her holes at the same time. She is moving back and forth so that he gets in deeper. Anna is an ass girl. She really loves being stuffed in this particular hole. Lucky for her, both these men are ass lovers too.

But Joe starts with her cunt. As she continues on Alan's cock, Joe's cock moves into her cunt deep. He thrusts hungrily into her, holding her firmly in place and making sure that she doesn't move around too much so that Alan's cock action isn't disturbed. Both men are caught exactly where they both want to be.

Anna pulls up off of Alan's dick and then goes for his balls. There she lathers his balls with hot sweat from her mouth. Her tongue glides easily over the surface of Alan's massive balls. Her hand moves up and down his shaft while her mouth works on his balls. Alan loves this ball action too.

Then his dick is back in her mouth, as Joe gets more determined on Anna's pussy. He really goes for it now as it is clear that his dick is hitting all the right places. He is really aiming to impress. His fingers are going into her ass with the same vigor as his cock is dealing with her pussy. Her mouth goes all the way down Alan's shaft, her gratitude for Joe's good job.

Then she lifts off of Alan again and straightens herself somewhat. Joe's fingers slip out of her ass but his dick stays put. She pushes Alan a little further onto the table and goes closer. She raises one leg onto the table. It goes so high because of her heel that Joe slips out of her cunt. Anna straddles Alan on her knees and replaces Joe's cock with Alan's in her pussy. Alan throws Joe a 'sorry' look.

But Joe isn't perturbed. He comes up against Anna's ass, standing between his buddy's legs. He eases his cock into Anna's ass and watches as she takes it all without even skipping a beat. Then she dances around on the dicks inside her, proving to both men that New York girls, and not California girls, are the best in bed. Both men meet her grinding with powerful thrusting and the three of them have soon forgotten where they are and why. Anna is starting to build up a considerable sweat, being taken to the edge of her limits by these two who have quite a powerful punch packed between their legs.

Alan stands up and Anna wraps tightly around his waist. He gets his positioning right and is fucking her with everything he's got. Joe goes deep and hard into her ass, helping Alan with the powerful cock he is pumping into her to keep her up. Alan is pushed hard against the table as Joe gets more and more aggressive, the sensations pumping into his cock from the hot ass he is fucking almost overwhelming him. Anna tastes as good as Alan and Joe have ever dared to imagine.

Then they are all standing again, Anna on her toes but not really holding herself up. She is fucked steadily from the front and the back as both men maintain perfect balance. Alan is getting closer and closer to cumming, Anna's pussy doing a great job of showing him where to go. Joe is enjoying her ass so much that he is willing himself not to cum yet, despite the ever-growing urge to.

When Alan is about to shoot, he apologizes to Anna and pulls out. She appreciates this courtesy but her pussy is furious, as she too was just about to blow. Joe sees the problem and pulls out of her ass. He swaps places with Alan and goes hard and fast into Anna's cunt. Again, he wills himself not to cum so that she does so first. With his dick stuffed deep inside her, he brings her back to where she was with Alan pretty fast.

Inside her ass, Alan is having a hard time holding back. He feels like there is less than a minute or so before he shoots into her. He asks for permission to do this. Anna can't answer, caught in her own orgasm already thanks to the precision of Joe's penis. He has really done well on her cunt while making sure that he doesn't shoot his load into her. But now she has cum, and she is incredibly happy. Alan has also cum, leaving Joe to pull the final curtain.

Alan has blown but his cock is still a little hard. Joe has a little request for the two of them. Alan is on his back on the table. Anna mounts him and after coaching his cock just a little so that it manages a path into her pussy. Then she leans forward so that her breasts are in direct contact with Alan's chest. Then Joe gets on top of her, which is essentially on top of both of them.

Anna expects his cock to slide into her ass but it doesn't. Joe's rock solid erection moves into her pussy right alongside Alan's softer meat. With the two dicks inside her Anna feels another orgasm fast approaching. Joe isn't concentrating on not cumming now, but on getting as close as possible inside Anna's cunt. It takes him ten minutes, Alan cumming just a little because his bags have mostly been empty. Anna has a completely explosive climax.

Then Joe pulls his cock from Anna, leaving Joe to enjoy the last bits of cunt energy she possesses. He drops into her ass full force and fucks her ass hard. This pushes Alan into the table so that his ass drags back and forth along the wooden surface. Joe's orgasm is loud and complete in every sense of the word. He fucks around with Alan by settling on Anna with his full weight. When Alan says he can't breathe, Joe removes his dick slowly and they all get dressed. It's almost six AM but they are suddenly ready to put their creative project to bed...

CHAPTER 3

THE LOCKUP... (RUSH HOUR!)

LUCIA IS TWENTY-ONE, hot, and very curious. She has always been one to meander on the risqué side of life. But she has managed to keep her rebellious, experimental side in check, especially since what people see is her ambitious, economist side that makes her look serious and ambitious. So since she started working for the largest Financial Advisory firm in Washington, she's been harboring a secret lust for their forty-year-old janitor, Dean.

Because of her mixed heritage, Japanese father, and American mother, she is as attractive to Dean, an African American with a large frame and an intense, interesting face, as she is to him. But Dean needs to keep his job, so he makes no obvious show of his lust for Lucia and some other attractive young, light-skinned girls who've come and gone through the building over the years he's been cleaning these offices.

When he pushes the door open just after five he isn't surprised to see Lucia fiddling with nothing at her desk. She's always the last to leave. Dean has always thought she was the most committed junior executive he's seen here in a while. She looks up at him when he greets her, returning the greeting with her perfect smile that exaggerates the slant of her eyes. He doesn't know what thoughts linger in her head, and she is unaware of his. So they move past each other as always, saying nothing further, and doing nothing. But today there seems to be a new intensity inside her pussy for his touch. She really wants him badly. What's the worst thing that could happen? Lucia has the kind of confidence that will make it easier for her to brush off his rejection.

She gets to the door, hearing Dean do what he does. She opens the door and then pushes it back closed. There is a quick catch on the door that locks it from the inside. Lucia listens to Dean work, turning bins out into his bag. She senses that he is watching her as she stands at the door. When he asks her if there's a problem, she turns the catch, locking the door with a loud snap.

Lucia turns around and places her laptop on the floor along with her purse. She removes her coat and walks toward Dean. His janitor instinct is overridden in seconds by his manhood. He knows by the way she is moving towards him, the way she is looking at him, that what she wants has nothing to do with the broom in his hand, and everything to do with the stick in his pants. He looks around for signs of a party, anything that will let him know that they've had a drink in the office. Nothing. She really just wants him.

She reaches him and places her lips on his, leaving his full mouth lined with gloss. He licks his lips, appreciating the taste of her balm. She pries the broom and the bag from his hands and zips his coveralls down to his waist. Then she slides it down off his shoulders and down his arms. Her hands move over his chest and she is impressed by his toned torso and thick, hard nipples. Then she runs her hands over his face, and his head, loving the traces of premature gray that dot his neatly trimmed hair. He clearly takes as much pride in himself as he does in his job.

Dean tries to speak, but each time she is silencing him with her lips. She doesn't want to mess this up with a conversation. It's just sex that she wants. And the bulge in Dean's pants suggests that he too isn't against the idea of sex. He can see from where he is standing that the catch on the door is indeed turned to locked. So as long as nobody from Lucia's office wants to come back to fetch a forgotten item, they have the place to themselves. But it's a Friday evening. And everybody has probably rushed to get as far away from work as possible.

When Dean's coveralls are gathered at his ankles, he has nothing but a tight vest and his boxers on. His cock is pushing against the soft cotton of his boxers, forming an impressive tent. Lucia pulls it off, freeing a massive fifteen-inch dick with a menacing thickness. Lucia knows already that she might have been a little ambitious here, this being the biggest dick she's ever presented herself with. But challenges are her thing. And it would also be incredibly unfair to expose this gentle giant like this and then leave him with nothing.

Dean watches her as she gets on her knees and sinks her nose between his legs. She smells his pubic hair and then takes a whiff of his nuts. She loves the smell of a man's groin. She runs her nose up and down Dean's shaft and then starts to lick the length of the tool. He pulls his foreskin back so that he can feel her tongue directly on the tip of his cock, already wanting to find the inside of Lucia's cunt. This is the last thing he expected. But it's not something that he hasn't allowed himself to fantasize about on occasion. He's pulled his dick many a night with images of Lucia running through his head.

Lucia opens her mouth over Dean's dick and starts to get it inside her. He bends his knees a little to help drop his dick into her mouth. She appreciates it and takes more of his cock into her mouth than she would normally have. Her ambition takes over and two-thirds of Dean's dick slides in and out of her mouth now easily. Dean groans loudly.

He watches Lucia enjoying his cock. He thrusts gently into her mouth, already stretched in a large circle. Her lips coat the cock in her mouth with the gloss coating them. She is really sucking on the ebony rod inside her mouth now, wanting to pull all its flavors into her mouth. Dean cannot believe that this is happening.

When she is licking his balls, Dean instinctively removes his vest. He pulls on his nipples hard. Dean's thrusts get a little carried away, fucking Lucia's hands that have both taken firm hold of his dick. He runs his fingers over the sensitive tip of his dick while Lucia devours his balls. Dean loves the fact that Lucia genuinely loves everything about his dick.

She brings herself to her feet and goes to where she dropped her bag. She feels around inside it and then comes out with a supersized Trojan. She can only hope that it will fit comfortably over the massive cock that hangs in front of Dean. He takes it from her and gets it over his dick easily. He asks her if she has any lube in there, checking his cock against Lucia's tiny waist. She has none.

Dean takes her in his arms and slides his hand under her skirt. He feels for where her underwear hugs her tightly, and pulls it down and then off. He unzips her skirt and helps her out of it. Then he takes her shirt off, one button at a time, and then removes her bra. He shakes his head at the perfection in front of him. He whispers in her ear, making sure that this is what she really wants. She really wants it.

He touches her cunt gently, teasing it with the tips of his fingers so that he stimulates her cunt to produce its own lube. He gets on his knees and parts her lips with his fingers, still gently, still not intrusive. He licks the inside of her pussy, tasting it, checking for moisture. It has started to sweat from the inside and so Dean goes in deeper with his tongue. Then he starts to finger her with one of his long, thick, strong fingers.

After getting her permission, he adds a second finger. She is more than willing and so he eases a second finger into her. He has the gentlest touch, tender and caring. He holds her up with one hand on her hip while he starts to go as deep into her with his two fingers inside her pussy. Lucia is responding well, Dean's fingers coming out wetter each time he sends them into her.

He continues to play with her clit and then fingers her as he gets to his feet. She is moaning now, begging him for his dick. Her hands are on his balls while he finishes up his preparations on her cunt. They need to figure out the best way to proceed. And Dean knows that it can only be one way, from his experience with women of Lucia's build.

Dean takes her to the wall, Lucia's hands against the firm surface and her legs parted. He pulls her back just a little so that he can reach under her and take her breasts in hand, and also so that he can move his hands over the front of her body while he takes care of her cunt from the back. After rubbing her cunt for a little while longer, he moves his cock into position and then starts to ease it into Lucia.

She has a great balance. But this doesn't mean that she isn't feeling the immense stretch from Dean's thick cock. He isn't in a hurry though, fucking her easily and tenderly with every inch that he manages to get inside her. As he thrusts into her, more and more of his dick getting further up inside, Lucia presses her head against the wall. She wills all his meat into her.

Dean is still not going to take her too quickly. He thrusts gently as he feeds her his dick an inch at a time. After a while, most of his cock is where Lucia wants it to be. Dean looks at his dick, happy with the length that Lucia's cunt has accommodated. It is clear however that she has no room inside her for more of his dick. So it's time to fuck her and to please her to the best of his ability.

His hands move around her and his fingers are on her clit. This is enough to have her cunt squeeze on his dick, almost sucking it deeper into herself. He thrusts all the way into her and then out, each thrust a little firmer than the one before it. This, coupled with the fingering on her clit, seals the satisfaction of being fucked by this man, making orgasm largely irrelevant.

Then she starts to move her ass backward, inviting him to go for her cunt with more power. She senses that his gentleness is more for her benefit than his. She starts to move firmly on his dick, pushing her cunt hard against him so that three more inches enter her. Dean goes harder and harder into her cunt, moving his cock from side to side as well so that he can widen her just a little more. This is the sensation that opens her unexpectedly and in a swift thrust, every single inch of Dean's thick, long meat slips into the tight pussy that feels like Christmas morning.

Dean seems to power his thrusts from his ankles all the way to his ass and then to his head, and all the way back down. He fucks Lucia smoothly in complete waves that send his cock all the way into her over and over again. This is exactly how she had imagined it. She rests her head against the wall and takes her fingers to her cunt while Dean holds onto her hips tightly. He doesn't skip a single beat as he brings her to a fucking awesome orgasm.

Her climax relaxes all the muscles in her body so that she can't stand up much longer. Dean eases them to the floor so that he is on his side, Lucia too, facing away from him. He goes back to his gentle strokes, taking his time fucking her for the thirty minutes it takes for him to finally cum. He eases out of her and then licks her cunt until it is clean and restored. She watches him sort out the condom as she gets dressed. Dean showers in the locker room and gets dressed in his jeans and vest. They go out for a drink to get to know each other a little better...

CHAPTER 4

THE GEEK AND I

I AM a hot blonde with an affinity for geeks. I know it sounds weird but I love them. They turn me on more than any other kind of man. You can have the jocks! I will choose a nerdy geek over a jock any day anytime. I have recently started working at a computer store in the office and I sat by a geek every day for 8 hours. It was complete sexual torture. Since I am the traditional blonde bimbo, he probably never even suspects that his rock-hard geek dick gets me wet every single day of the week.

It was a secret I had kept for far too long to myself. It was time that I showed this geek just how much he turned me on. On this particular day, I had taken extra time to look my hottest and my absolute sexiest. There was no way the computer boy was going to be able to resist me in the red mini skirt and sheer silk top I had worn especially for him today. I walked into my cubicle area and saw my handsome geek at work quickly typing codes into his PC. My God, he turned me on when he did that. I even liked seeing his long nimble fingers push his glasses up to his nose so he could see his screen better. "Hello Melvin," I said seductively as I swung my ass close to his face and bent down to pick up the pencil I had dropped on purpose. "Err...hello Brittany," he said back sheepishly.

"Melvin would you be a dear and come help me with this anti-virus program. I cannot seem to get it to work right," I said as I bent over to show Melvin my ample and pulsating cleavage. I could feel my hot tits get hard underneath my white blouse that if it was any thinner would be see-through. "Uh...uh, okay sure," said Melvin getting up from his ergonomic chair to reveal an explosive boner growing in his tan khakis. I looked down and my baby blues grew wide with pleasure. I licked my lips whether out of habit or on purpose, I am not completely certain.

I swear I saw beads of sweat forming on Melvin's brow as he clicked away on my keyboard as I wished his fingers were flicking my hot bud between my legs. "How about you and I go have some lunch today Melvin? I'll treat you since you are helping me out." I said longingly. "Okay sure," He replied shyly. Melvin seemed nervous but his boner was raring and ready to go. I could see it lying next to his zipper dying to emerge into the light of day and probably deep inside my bald cunt. The next few hours passed quickly and it finally became time for me to seduce Melvin on the way to lunch. Little did he know I had gotten approval for him and I to take the rest of the day off for some "computer" repair.

When I pulled into my driveway, I saw the look of complete surprise on Melvin's face. "Don't worry Melvin. This is my house. I wanted to surprise you. I asked Mr. Ditmeir to let us have the day off for some home computer repairs. He happily agreed. I will take good care of you. Don't you worry," I said as I chuckled seductively. Melvin and I went inside my house. I told Melvin to make himself comfortable on my mauve-colored sofa lined with laced pillows. Melvin looked so fucking hot with his dick dying to pop out of his khakis. He picked up a lacy pillow and tried to hide his boner but I could still see the impression of his cock rim through the thin fabric.

I got Melvin and me a glass of chilled chardonnay and sat down next to him on the sofa. Melvin tried to inch away from me but I kept scooting closer until he had nowhere to go. Let's just say Melvin was trapped between a rock and a hard place. I looked at Melvin and then reached in to kiss his cheek. He giggled and pushed his glasses up to the bridge of his nose. "Melvin, why don't I take those specs from you?" I said as I reached in to do so I planted my cleavage right in his eyes.

I decided that it was time to turn up the heat a notch or two on Melvin. So I decided to take the initiative. I wasn't waiting any longer. And to Melvin's surprise and a little bit to my own, I kissed him. I don't mean I laid a small peck on his cheek, I really laid a hot kiss on him. It didn't take long and Melvin was returning my wet kiss with vengeance. He even began to grab my tits and pull them from their restraints. I pulled the left one up myself and stuck it into Melvin's hungry mouth. He removed his glasses and began to suckle my tit ferociously. It seemed to me that behind his geek exterior resided an animal in Melvin.

Before I could say a word, Melvin was ripping my skirt down and backing me up against the wall. I reached for his zipper and out sprung a long hard-as-steel cock. I guided it deep inside my pussy. He plunged inside me with one big thrust. I winced in animal pleasure. He had a long hard boner that wouldn't stop as he fucked me hard up against the wall. This was the best fuck I had ever had in my life!

We took our screwing to the bedroom and we fucked for

a solid two hours. I came all over his dick and Melvin unloaded his seed hard inside of me. I then pushed him between my legs and he ate the fuck out of my cunt I thrust my hips hard up to his mouth and once again unloaded my cream all over his face until it dripped down his chin. Melvin and I had a great afternoon and evening fucking and sucking and we continued to be fuck buddies for months afterward. It just goes to show you can never underestimate the power of a geek.

CHAPTER 5

THE NEW GIRL IN THE OFFICE (OFFICE SEX)

GINGER ADAMS HAD FINALLY DONE it. She had finally landed her dream job. She was the new partner at the Ferguson Law Firm. She had gone through the long process of becoming a lawyer. It seemed that no law firm was willing to give her a fighting chance. Finally, Greg Ferguson saw something in her that made him want to allow her the opportunity to become a member of the Ferguson Law Firm. Ginger got up and was ready to go on her first day. Something in the air told her that her life was going to be going in the right direction. Ginger made her way to the office building. It was a rather odd-shaped building and the first time that she had visited, she got lost a couple of times before she was able to get where she needed to go. The security guard who was working the desk saw Ginger, saw her Ferguson Law Firm badge, and welcomed her. The security guard introduced herself as Maybelline and told Ginger that if she needed anything to not hesitate and to let her know. Ginger headed up to the floor that the Firm was on and walked into the office. There were a number of faces that stopped and looked at her as if she were the new kid in class. Ginger felt uncomfortable before the owner Greg Ferguson made his way out of his office and greeted Ginger as he introduced her to the rest of the lawyers and the partners.

Greg had Ginger start off by getting accustomed to the layout of the office. One of these floors included the mock courtroom that was designed to help prep new lawyers and witnesses who were needed to testify in a court case. Ginger was assigned the task of going up there and making sure everything was perfect as they had a big case that was going to be tried. They needed to make sure that all details were in place before they got underway. Ginger was in the courtroom getting things in place when Greg walked in and closed the door behind him. Greg walked in and came over to where she was working.

"Ginger, come here, I want to talk to you for a few minutes. I have some things that I want to get off my chest if you don't mind. You know why we brought you on to be a member of the law firm, don't you? It is simply because of your body. Let's face it; you are a young female lawyer. You have about as much real-world experience as a newbie college student. I took one look at you when you came in to interview and I knew that you were going to make for a fine piece of ass here in the office. You are not going to be a lawyer here, you are simply going to be the in-house whore. For that, you will get a very nice salary and will want for nothing. I can't sit here and bullshit you. The guys in the office are going to be looking to get their pricks into you and fuck you as hard as they can. The truth is that this courtroom is never used for anything except the guys of the firm to bring their women up here and fuck them. It is secluded, quiet and no one ever bothers you. The last girl that worked in here left because she got tired of being picked and probed by the men. I hated to see her leave, but a good redhead may be a good addition to the office. I get worked up at the thought of you and me having wild sex in here. Why don't you and I get to know one another a little better? Get that fine ass of yours here so I can see you closer."

Ginger walked over to where Greg was sitting. Greg took his hand and began to caress the outside of Ginger's breasts under her top. Ginger began to unbutton it. Ginger was not really offended by the fact that Greg wanted to fuck her. She was excited by the fact that she actually had a good job and since she loved to have sex, this was a perfect situation for her. Ginger took her bra off and allowed her tits to fall from her bra and to be exposed. Greg reached up and began to squeeze and pull on her nipples.

Reaching over to her purse, Ginger took the lighter out and lit it. She allowed the flame to dance around her nipples barely touching the nipples. Ginger got off on this and when Greg reached up under the skirt, he discovered that Ginger's panties were soaked.

Ginger got onto her knees and prepared herself for Greg to insert his cock into her mouth for her to nurse on and suck on. Ginger had gotten through her first year of college by sucking off half of her professors for her grades. Then she discovered that money worked as well and just began to pay them off. Ginger was a cock hound and she had perfected the hunt to perfection. Taking the end of Greg's cock, she began to nurse on it. He took his head and slid it down her throat. Ginger did not gag at all and took the entire length down her throat. Ginger loved the taste of cock and did not mind the sensation of having her throat abused with a large, uncut cock. Ginger pulled off and leaned back a little bit so as to allow him the chance to take his jizz and plant it on her tits the white streams hit her dark brown areolas and made quite a contrast. Ginger loved the sensation of cum hitting her tits. There was something about this that made her get hot and bothered and cum almost on command. Ginger had an eruption shoot from her slit that went all over the floor and made quite a mess.

The rest of the time Greg and Ginger fucked in various places located in the courtroom. Ginger was not one to admit this openly, as she wanted to give a little of an impression that she was doing this under duress, but Ginger actually had one of the most amazing orgasms that she had ever had. Ginger had a feeling inside of her gut that she was going to like the new positions or positions that she was taking with the Ferguson Law Firm. Being a slut has its advantages, and Ginger was determined that she was going to make the most of it.

ABOUT THE AUTHOR

Danika Falls is an emerging erotica author of many erotica kinks and sub-genres. Be sure to check out other books and leave a review if this story got you hot!

Visit my blog at Danika Falls Blog

Join my newsletter for the exclusive Danika Falls Newsletter

Sign up for Free Stories from Xplicit Press Authors

Xplicit Press Author Updates

Like Xplicit Press on Facebook

Follow Xplicit Press on Twitter

Readers: I want to expand a few of the stories to see where the characters can be explored further. If there are any of the stories that you would like to read more about again, I'd love to hear from you!

Keep In Touch
Danika Falls
info@danikafalls.com